With special thanks to Conrad Mason

For Arthur Mason

ORCHARD BOOKS

First published in Great Britain in 2021 by The Watts Publishing Group

1 3 5 7 9 10 8 6 4 2

Text © Beast Quest Limited 2021
Cover and inside illustrations by Juan Calle
© Beast Quest Limited 2021
Illustration: Juan Calle (Liberum Donum). Cover colour: Santiago Calle.
Shading: Juan Calle and Luis Suarez

Series created by Beast Quest Limited, London

A CIP catalogue record for this book is available from the British Library.

ISBN 978 1 40835 791 0

Printed in Great Britain

Orchard Books
An imprint of Hachette Children's Group
Part of The Watts Publishing Group Limited
Carmelite House, 50 Victoria Embankment, London EC4Y 0DZ

An Hachette UK Company
www.hachette.co.uk
www.hachettechildrens.co.uk

MONSTER
FROM THE VOID

ADAM BLADE

ORCHARD

Avantia ...

Once upon a time, it was a lush, green planet with sparkling blue oceans. A haven for life in all its forms, and a home to eight billion people. A place of incredible technology and culture.

Until the Void ...

In Avantia City, it struck on a clear day at the height of summer. No one saw it coming. No one understood it. And no one was prepared.

First there was a roar, like distant thunder. Then a swirling vortex ripped apart the sky, streaked with vivid green and purple storms of electricity. It was vast, like the mouth of a monster.

As earthquakes shook the ground, the citizens scrambled into any craft that could fly. They fled their homes, their very atmosphere … and from the darkness of space, they watched the Void swallow their planet, leaving nothing behind.

For most, it was the end.

But for those lucky few, the survivors …

It was only the beginning.

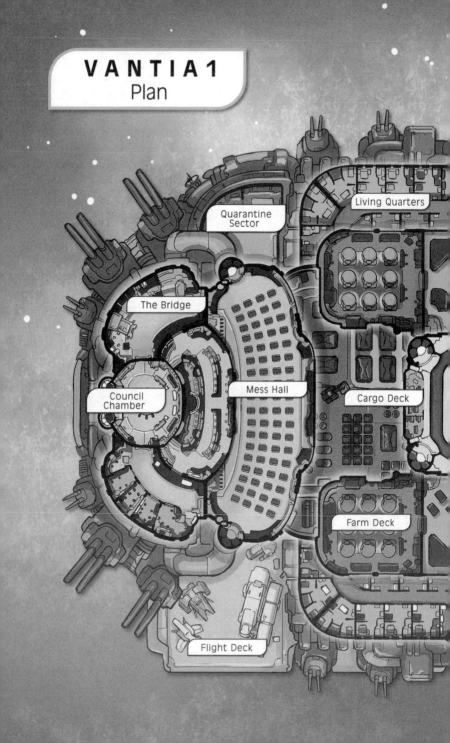

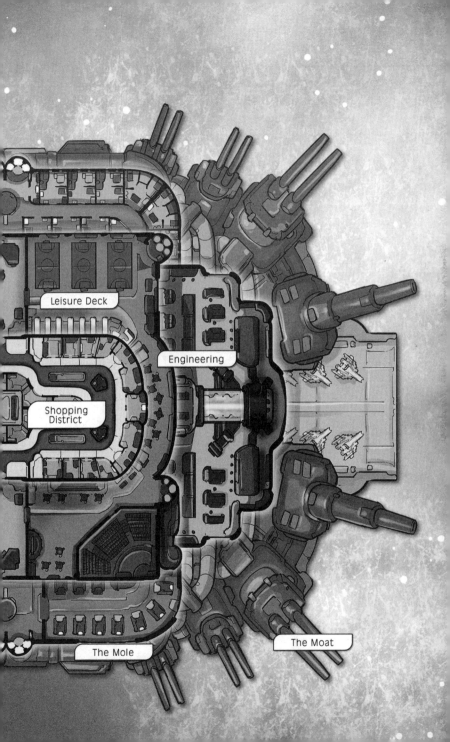

Leisure Deck

Engineering

Shopping
District

The Mole

The Moat

1: *Harry Hugo* is a talented apprentice engineer, and there's nothing he can't fix.

2: *Ava Achebe* is a cadet, training to be one of Vantia1's elite space pilots.

3: *Zo Harkman*, Chief Engineer, has taken care of Harry ever since his parents disappeared.

4: *Markus Knox*, another cadet, *thinks* he's brave and daring ...

5: *Governor Knox* is in charge of running Vantia1 and protecting all the station's inhabitants.

6: *Admiral Achebe* is the commander of the space fleet, and gives orders to the pilots.

CONTENTS

CHAPTER 1

NAVAL TACTICS

Two teams of cadets floated in the zero-G game chamber, all at angles to one another. Without any gravity, there was no up or down. It reminded Harry Hugo of deep space itself.

But there was no time to think about that right now.

"Catch!" yelled Ava. She flung the ball, and it spun through the air in a flash of silver.

"Got it," muttered Harry.

He had wired his prosthetic arm up to his rocket boots, and a twitch of his thumb rerouted power to the thrusters. A little too much power. *WHOOOSH!* His heart lurched as he shot off, straight past the ball towards the metal wall of the game chamber.

He was too slow to manoeuvre and threw up his arms just in

time to cushion the impact. *THUMP!*

Laughter echoed round the chamber as he righted himself. He saw a tall, blond-haired boy in the other team's colours intercept Ava's pass. *Markus Knox.* Harry gritted his teeth as his smug opponent flipped in the air, then hurled the ball towards the goal. The keeper flailed but failed to stop it.

"GOOOOAL!" The cry rang around the chamber. The glow-buoys flashed green and Markus did a victory somersault. A holographic scoreboard spun slowly above the court. *8-0.*

Harry groaned. Zero-G handball took some getting used to – especially with a new pair of rocket boots.

"Hey Robo-arm, nice catch!" crowed Markus. He looped the loop, and Harry noticed that he was wearing Fireflash Rocket Hoppers – the best boots that credits could buy. *Boots I'd never be able to afford ...*

"Pro tip," called Markus. "In the cadets, we try *not* to fly straight into walls." He grinned at his team-mates, but none of them seemed to find him all that funny.

Harry clenched his fists. His cheeks burned. But before he could answer back, Ava's hand closed over his arm. "Hey! You're new to the cadets, remember? This is the first time you've even played. You're doing great." Harry felt a little calmer, looking into her kind brown eyes. But he could still hear Markus behind her.

"And check out those boots! I've seen cheap fakes before, but seriously ... They look home-made!"

"They are," snapped Harry, before Ava could stop him. "Not everyone on Vantia1 has more credits than sense."

He was rewarded with a brief flash of anger on his rival's face. Markus might be the Governor's son, but Harry knew that making rocket boots from scratch was *way* beyond him.

Then, luckily, the scoreboard chimed and rose up through a hatch in the ceiling. It was the end of the match.

Zero-G deactivated, and the players all sank slowly to the bottom of the chamber.

✪

"Seriously, it wasn't that bad," said Ava a little while later, as they took off their rocket boots in the cadets' common room. "My first zero-G match, I spent half of it spinning round and round in circles. I got so dizzy I threw up afterwards!"

Harry grinned. "I'm fine," he said. "To be honest … I was finding it hard to concentrate on the game."

Ava's grin faded, and she nodded. She must have guessed what was on Harry's mind.

Vellis. Harry couldn't get the man out of his head. Vellis, with his sneering smile and his arrogant gaze ... Vellis, the scientist who had tried to destroy Vantia1 with a huge, powerful robo-dragon. Vellis, who had worked with Harry's parents back on their home world of Avantia, before the spinning vortex known as the Void had swallowed the whole planet, and Harry's parents with it ...

Vantia1's analysts had always blamed Harry's mum and dad for the Void. They said his parents had created it by accident, in a scientific experiment gone wrong. But Harry *knew* it wasn't their fault. And if he could just prove it was Vellis who was responsible ...

He realised he was clenching his fists again, and forced himself to relax.

Captain Nyman stepped into the room. The leader of the Cadet Force stood ramrod-straight in his purple uniform, gold braid glittering on his shoulders and chest. He was tall and stern, and his sweep of glossy black hair was streaked with grey. "Look sharp, cadets," he said. "Only five hours until the history test. Get changed and get cramming."

Ava rolled her eyes at Harry when Captain Nyman turned away. Harry grinned. He knew she would ace the test. Her mother was Admiral Achebe, after all, and the test was on naval tactics throughout the ages.

Behind them, Markus was whispering

to his gang. "Who cares about history? We're on the most advanced space station ever created, and Captain No-fun wants us to learn about *wooden boats*."

"I certainly do, Cadet Knox," said Captain Nyman, calmly.

Harry couldn't help smiling as he saw the blood drain from Markus's face. Nyman's excellent hearing was legendary.

"Sorry, sir," mumbled Markus.

"You will be, if you don't study," said Captain Nyman. "If we don't learn from the past, we only make the same mistakes over and over. Remember that, Knox. And I'll see all of you in ..." He checked a screen on his wrist. "... four hours, fifty-eight minutes … and forty-four seconds." He turned on his heel and marched away.

"You can wipe that smile off your face, loser," Markus snarled at Harry. "You owe me a week's candy rations, remember?"

Ava raised an eyebrow.

"We had a bet on the game," explained Harry, with a sigh. "Big mistake, obviously."

"Deck 5," said a smooth, automated voice, a few minutes later. The metal doors of the Mole transport system slid open, and Harry stepped out of the pod. There were countless pods in Vantia1, all criss-crossing the station in a network of twisting tunnels.

Through a long viewing window, Harry could see the darkness of space, framed by the edge of Vantia1. The hull stretched out into the distance, like a vast cliff made of glittering metal.

Normally it was a comforting sight – a reminder of the fortress-like strength of the space station. Vantia1 had been built as a safe haven – a refuge for the people of Avantia, after their planet was destroyed. But it wasn't long since the robo-dragon had attacked the station, and now the hull was scarred with gaping rips and exposed struts. TechDroids darted across the damaged sections like swarms of bees, their robotic arms swivelling, welding and fixing new sheets of metal into place.

That robo-dragon nearly finished us off, thought Harry, with a shudder.

He carried on down the corridor, heading for his quarters. Several engineers were clustered around a console, hard at work, and as Harry passed, a big man with a shaved head caught his eye and winked.

"Off to polish your boots again, Hazza?"

Harry grinned at the familiar face. It was Farooq, one of his old friends from his days as an engineering apprentice. "You offering to do it for me?" he asked.

Farooq flashed a grin
full of gold teeth.
"Ha! You cadets
should try doing
some *real* work
once in a while."
He frowned.
"Seriously, Hazza,
when are you going
to come and visit your old buddies in
Engineering? It's been too long."

Harry couldn't meet Farooq's eye. He
felt suddenly very aware of the man's
grease-stained overalls, and of his own
brand-new purple and gold uniform. "I
keep meaning to. There's just so much
stuff to learn. And drills, and—"

"I get it," said Farooq, waving a hand. "No big deal." Harry wasn't sure he really *did* get it. He felt a squirm of guilt.

"Just don't forget us when you make Admiral, OK?" Farooq laughed and turned back to his fellow engineers.

Harry smiled awkwardly, but his friend was already hard at work again. He hurried on, keeping his head down.

Harry's quarters were at the end of the corridor. He entered the passcode, waiting for the buzz and click of the door unlocking. But the door stayed shut. *Huh.*

He pushed his ear up against the metal. Inside he could hear the scuffling of feet, and the scraping of heavy objects being pulled across the floor.

"Zo?" he called. "Are you in there?" Zo Harkman was Vantia1's Head of Engineering, and Harry's guardian. Back on Avantia, he'd been a good friend of Harry's parents. It was funny, though – he didn't often double-lock the door to their shared quarters.

Beep! The door slid suddenly open, making Harry stumble off balance.

"Ah – there you are!" Zo Harkman had a wild look in his eyes, and his normally neatly combed grey hair was sticking up at an angle, as though he'd been running his hands through it.

"Everything all right?" asked Harry.

"Of course. Why do you ask?"

"Er ..." said Harry.

"Cadets – how was it?" asked Zo, as though he'd only just remembered. He stepped aside, so that Harry could enter.

Harry's eyes darted around the neat, minimal white furniture of the living space, hoping for some clue about what Zo was up to. But everything was just as it should be. *Maybe it was nothing after all.*

He threw himself on to the sofa, and felt his body sag with exhaustion. He was suddenly feeling very tired. "It was fine," he said. "Well, actually …" He licked his lips. "It's pretty hard. Captain Nyman doesn't go easy."

Zo settled into an armchair. "Nothing worthwhile is easy."

Harry reached for a bowl on a side table, then thought better of it. The food production biomes were still out of action after Vellis's attack, so the bowl was full of long-life nutrient algae. The slimy brown cubes weren't exactly appetising. He sighed.

"What's up, Harry?" said Zo, gently. "Are you thinking about the attack?"

Harry nodded. "And my parents."

Zo's face fell at that. Harry knew he hated talking about this. After all, there was nothing Zo could say to bring them back. *But still* ... "If there's a chance they're alive, even the smallest—"

"Harry ..." Zo leaned forward and laid a firm hand on his arm. "Some things can't be changed – and what can't be changed must be accepted."

"*Accepted?*" Harry couldn't help the bitterness creeping into his voice. "So I'm supposed to just *accept* that they're gone? Accept that everyone blames them for the Void? For what happened to Avantia?" His voice was rising, and he stood. "If you really cared about them – if you cared about me—"

"Don't you dare, Harry!"

Harry was caught off guard by the fierceness in his guardian's voice. Zo's blue eyes were blazing, and he jabbed at his palm with a finger. "For eight years, I've looked after you as if you were my own! And now you tell me I don't *care*?"

Harry felt anger surging through his own body as he stood up. He couldn't believe how quickly the argument had blown up. But he didn't know how to end it, either. "Well, if I'm such a burden, you can stop right now!"

He stormed to his bedroom. If he could have slammed the door, he would have. But instead he punched the lock code fiercely into the pad, and let the door slide smoothly shut behind him.

SNOOPING

Harry's communicator bleeped with an alert. *Two hours until the history test.*

He shot a glance at the holo-board on his bedroom wall, where 3D scans of old history books were hovering – books that Zo had brought with him from Avantia. *I should so be studying right now.* But he hadn't read a single page.

He sighed and turned back to the task that had kept him busy for the last few hours. His Space Stallion was propped up on a metal frame, taking up most of the floor space in his room. Harry was exhausted and covered in grease, but the Stallion was finally fixed. He'd hammered the twisted, half-melted chassis back into shape, replaced the busted screens, rewired the scrambled circuits … Vellis's robo-dragon had really done a number on it.

Taking a deep breath, Harry thumbed the ID pad. With a juddering whirr of fans, the Stallion rose up into the air,

LEDs blinking across its chrome body. "How-how-howdy, H," said the Stallion, in its familiar cowboy drawl. "Howdy. Howdy. Howdy. Howdy."

Just the voice chip left to replace. "Get some rest, buddy," said Harry, and shut the Stallion down again.

He would need to go to the labs to get a new voice chip. But that would mean getting Zo's permission, and after the fight, Harry was in no mood to talk to him.

Tiptoeing across the room, he pressed his ear against the wall. He could just about hear Zo snoring soundly in the room next door.

Well, it would be rude to wake him,

wouldn't it?

Slipping out of his bedroom, Harry silently slid Zo's security pass from the dining table and hung it round his own neck.

✪

Taking the Mole to Deck 4, Harry got a familiar rush of excitement as he slotted the pass into a reader and stepped into Zo Harkman's private lab. Harry loved the place, and it reminded him immediately of all the great times he'd had tinkering alongside his guardian.

His eyes darted across the labyrinth of glass cubicles, the state-of-the-art consoles lining the walls, the pristine white diagnostic slabs and gleaming

vidscreens … And above all, the *tech* –
racks of robotic operating limbs, power
cutters, welding tools …

No time to linger. Harry crossed the
lab to the chip bank and drew up the
very latest voice chip – one that Harkman
had designed himself.

He was just turning to leave when he
started, heart pumping. The door to the
store-room at the side of the lab that
had been left unlocked. A figure was
standing perfectly still inside. Watching
him.

"Hello?" said Harry. The figure didn't
move. And when Harry peered closer,
he saw that it wasn't a person at all, but
some sort of spacesuit.

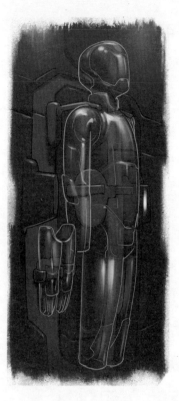

Harry edged closer, and stepped into the small room. It wasn't like any space suit he'd ever seen before. It was transparent, made from a strange material that glistened like a slug trail.

A pair of gloves made of the same material hung beside the suit. Harry took one and slipped his hand inside, flexing his fingers. It felt weird – soft yet strong at the same time. *What in the name of Avantia is it for?*

A shadow fell over him.

"Unauthorised intruder!"

Harry's heart leapt into his mouth. Spinning round, he saw a security droid hovering in the corner of the room, blue eyes glowing in its blank white face. A disruptor-ray barrel slid smoothly out of its chest, pointing straight at Harry.

"Whoa there." Harry raised his hands. "It's me, Harry. I live with Zo ..."

"Only Dr Harkman is authorised for entry," said the droid.

Harry blinked. Whatever this room was – whatever the spacesuit was – Zo hadn't mentioned it to him. Which was odd. Zo *loved* talking about his engineering projects. Half the time, Harry had to beg him to stop.

Harry tried to edge past the droid, but it moved in tandem, the glowing disruptor trained on him. Harry licked his lips. "Easy does it!"

"Harry? What are you *doing* here?"

Zo stood in the doorway.

Harry's heart sank. "I just … I came for a voice chip. But you must have left this door unlocked because—"

"And you took my pass, too?"

"Unauthorised intruder!" said the droid again.

Zo thumbed a pad on the droid's head. Its weapon slid away, its eyes powered down and it lowered gently to the floor again.

When he turned back to Harry, Zo's shock had turned to anger. "This isn't the first time you've been snooping around, Harry."

"I wasn't *snooping*!" Harry exploded. "And I'm not the one keeping secrets." He pointed at the space suit. "What is this thing?"

Zo's jaw clenched tight. His eyes darted around, and suddenly Harry felt as if it was he who had caught his guardian out.

"It's nothing important," said Zo, at last. *He always was a terrible liar.*

"Then it won't matter if you tell me what it is," said Harry.

"You don't understand, Harry. Some

things you aren't *ready* to understand."

But before Harry could ask what *that* was supposed to mean, Harkman's communicator chimed. "Chief Engineer Harkman, report to the Bridge at once."

Zo sighed. "We'll finish this later, all right?"

Harry shook his head. "I'm coming with you. Unless this is another thing I'm not *ready to understand*?"

His guardian threw up his hands.

Well, it's not a "no", thought Harry.

✪

A few minutes later, they stepped out of the Mole and on to the Observation Deck, otherwise known as the Bridge.

The vast transparent dome at the very

top of Vantia1 was bustling with activity. Observation technicians manned banks of consoles, all talking rapidly into their headsets. On the platform in the centre of the Bridge was Admiral Achebe in her military uniform, leaning in close to talk to Governor Knox, who sat in her command chair, hawk-like eyes fixed on the main screen. Beside them stood the figure of Secretary Bremmer, the chief assistant to the Governor.

Harry whistled. "Something's really up."

Zo nodded.

A.D.U.R.O. was there too. The holographic face of the station's artificial intelligence hovered in mid-air above the

command chair. It was the size of a small transport vessel, young and female, with spiky white hair. As always, it watched everything with total calm – not the slightest trace of emotion.

"Harkman!" Governor Knox had spotted them and beckoned them up on to the platform. "We have a little problem." The Governor had the same bright blue eyes and the same natural air of command as her son. But unlike Markus, she had earned it.

"There's an incoming asteroid," said Admiral Achebe briskly. "Initial scans suggest it's half the size of the station. Impact in two hours and forty-seven minutes."

Zo frowned. "But that's impossible. Long-range sensors would have picked it up well before now."

"They did." A.D.U.R.O.'s gentle voice was every bit as calm as her features. "Unfortunately, the asteroid has changed trajectory."

"Asteroids don't do that," said Harry, without thinking. "They follow an orbit."

Secretary Bremmer glared at him. He was dressed in black, as usual. Bremmer was a short man, with a short temper to match. "Well, this one has. Chief Engineer Harkman, what is your boy doing on the Bridge?"

"Never mind that." Governor Knox waved a dismissive hand. "Harkman, what do you suggest?"

"Something must be interfering with the asteroid's path," Zo muttered, peering at the screen of an Ob Tech. "I wonder ..." He shook his head and turned to the Governor. "Let's engage main thrusters," he said. "Move the whole station."

Governor Knox nodded. "A.D.U.R.O.?"

"Engaging thrusters," said the AI.

The deck thrummed beneath them, and Harry felt the vibrations run right through his feet. Then – *CLUNK* – there was a jolt, and several officers stumbled. The vibrations died entirely.

"What was that?" asked the Admiral sharply.

Lights flickered across the Bridge. Several Ob Techs cast nervous glances around the room.

"We're not moving," said Governor Knox.

"Correct," said A.D.U.R.O. evenly. "Thrusters are down. Cause unknown."

"So what does that mean?" spluttered Secretary Bremmer.

"It means we're a sitting duck," growled Zo.

"Indeed," said A.D.U.R.O. "Total annihilation of Vantia1, in T-minus 2 hours and 44 minutes. Shall I commence countdown?"

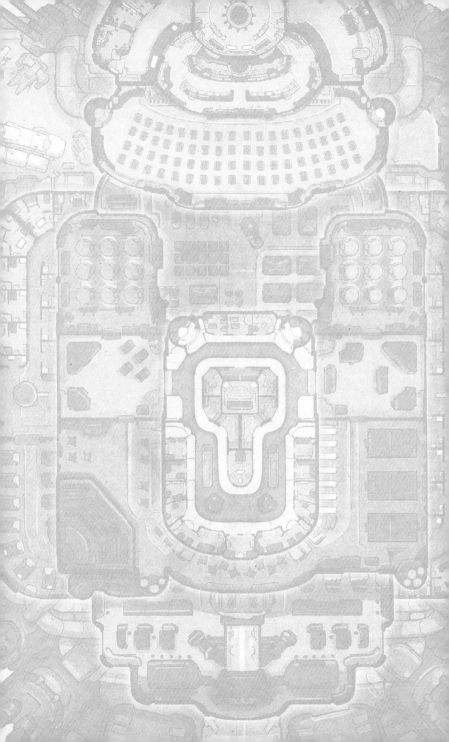

THE POWER CORE

The Bridge was buzzing as the Ob
Techs worked at double speed, trying to
locate the problem that had disabled the
thrusters. Each time they tried to reboot
the system, A.D.U.R.O. announced it had
failed.

Harry couldn't help himself. "It's the

robo-dragon," he said. "It caused so much damage …"

"Harry!" said Zo, sternly.

"But the boy's right, isn't he?" said Governor Knox.

Zo hesitated, then nodded. "I should say so. The power core is still severely compromised. If reboots don't work, we'll only have one option."

"Reboot 04 has failed," said A.D.U.R.O.

Admiral Achebe groaned. "What was that one option, Harkman?"

Zo rolled up his sleeves. "I'll have to get down there myself, fix this the old-fashioned way."

Can I come too? Harry was about to ask. But to his surprise, Zo laid a hand on his shoulder. "You're with me, Harry."

The Admiral raised an eyebrow. "A cadet? With level one clearance? Down in the power core?"

"I'll keep an eye on him," said Zo. "And let's not forget, it was thanks to Harry that Vantia1 survived the attack of the robo-dragon."

Harry's heart swelled with pride. So their arguments were forgotten. All was forgiven. In fact, it was the nicest thing his guardian had said to him since—

"Quickly!" snapped Zo, already striding off. "No time to dawdle."

✪

The Mole doors slid open on Deck 7, and Harry and Zo stepped out on to a metal walkway. They'd stopped only to pick up a toolbox. At the end of the walkway was the highest security door that Harry had ever seen. He'd read the specs – it was made of specially treated solid fernium, several centimetres thick.

He watched, holding his breath, as Zo went through the access protocols. Retinal scan … Thumb print … Entry code …

Hssssss! The door swung slowly open, and a soft red glow spilled from inside.

"Coming?" called Zo, over his shoulder.

Harry followed his guardian into a small antechamber, lined with more gleaming fernium. Harry felt like he was in a submarine from ancient times, back on Avantia.

The thought reminded him of the homework he wasn't doing. *Never mind – some things are definitely more important than revision.*

Zo was already pulling on a stiff, rubberised anti-radiation suit. He tossed one to Harry.

"Remember, the radiation in there is lethal," said Zo. "Without these suits, we'd be dead in seconds." He had never been one to mince his words.

"I get it," said Harry. He donned the suit, and was just about to pull on his helmet when Zo laid a hand on his arm.

"Just one moment." Turning, Zo

punched a code into the panel by
the access door, and it hissed shut.
They were alone, sealed off in the

antechamber. There
was a funny look in
Zo's eye – a secretive,
almost frightened
look.

"Can you, er …
can you keep a
secret?" he asked.

Harry felt the hairs
rise at the back of his
neck. He nodded.

"Good." Zo sat on
a bench at the edge of the room. His
fingers were drumming on his knees.

Harry didn't think he'd ever seen him so agitated. "This is the only place on Vantia1 where we can't be overheard. Even A.D.U.R.O. doesn't monitor this room."

Harry held his breath. He felt as though he were on the edge of some huge, terrifying discovery. And he wasn't sure yet if it was a discovery he wanted to make.

"The truth is ..." Zo sighed. "I've been carrying out experiments – *unauthorised* ones. I've been sending organic material into – and out of – the Void."

Harry gasped. This had to be the first time his guardian had ever broken a rule in his life. But that wasn't what had sent the adrenaline surging through Harry's body …

"That suit," he said. "The one I saw in your secret room, in the lab. That's what it's for!"

Zo held up a firm hand. "It's early days, Harry," he said. "Please don't get carried away." But he couldn't hide the gleam of excitement in his own eyes. "I've tested the material with some plants, enclosed them and sent them into the Void. The first few times they just came back as sludge, but the last times – well, they came back in one piece."

"If it works for plants, it'll work for a human!" said Harry.

"It's too soon," said Zo firmly. "I don't know the long-term effects."

Harry couldn't believe what he was hearing. No one knew what lay inside the Void. It was just... the Void. But this invention could change all that. "I don't understand," he said. "Why keep this secret?"

Zo frowned. "A few weeks back, after the robo-dragon attack, someone tried to hack into my data files. I couldn't trace it. But it made me wonder ... what if Vellis has a mole inside Vantia1? A spy on board the station."

Harry nodded. *That explains the security droid, back in the lab.* He felt a fresh rush of pride that Zo was sharing all of this with him. *He trusts me.*

"Not a word of this to anyone," said his guardian. "Now – helmets on."

They secured their helmets. Then Zo entered a code into a pad on the other side of the chamber, and the door to the power core slid smoothly open.

Bright red light flooded the chamber, and a wall of heat hit them. Harry felt his boots leave the floor. The station's gravity systems were disabled here, and they floated free, swimming into the power core chamber with bursts of thrust from the soles of their boots.

Harry had seen the core once before, when it had been exposed in the fight with the robo-dragon – but never up

close, like this. It was
a gigantic red orb,
so bright it hurt to
look at, held in place
with a clutter of struts
and cables.

"Goggles," said Zo,
through the in-suit comms.
Switches at their suit wrists tinted their
visors like sunglasses, so that the power
core became a much dimmer red. Now
Harry could see that the core's rounded
surface was actually made of thousands
of individual fuel cells clustered together.

"There!" he said, pointing. At the top
of the chamber, a cable was drifting free
from its connection.

"That'll be the problem," said Zo. "We'll sort that in no time."

They swam up through the core chamber. But as they got closer, Harry squinted at the cable. "Wait, that's …"

"Cut," finished Zo, grimly. "It's been sabotaged."

The cable was as thick as a wrist, bulky and tightly wound. But it was severed all the way through, the ends burned, as though by some kind of power tool.

Vellis's mole. It has to be.

"You hold it together while I seal it," said Zo. Harry connected the two burned ends, while Zo got to work with a welding tool. In seconds the job was done.

Zo opened a comms channel to the Bridge. "Thrusters should be working now, Governor. But we should restart the system and run diagnostics first. I'm sorry to say it looks like deliberate damage."

But it was Secretary Bremmer's voice that crackled through the communicator. "Understood. Stand down now, Harkman."

"That's all the thanks we get?" said Harry, frowning. "He didn't sound very surprised!"

Zo smiled. "He always was a frosty one."

They returned to the antechamber, the door sliding shut behind them. Harry realised he'd been sweating, and he was glad to be away from the heat of the power core. The rubber suit wasn't helping, and he peeled it off as quickly as he could.

"That was good work, Harry," said Zo, as he hung up their suits and entered the pass code to leave the chamber. "Good, honest engineering. Nothing like it for …"

As the door hissed open, he trailed off. He stared.

Harry followed his gaze, and a jolt of shock ran through him.

The corridor beyond was full of security guards, heavily armed with blasters. Every one of them was pointing at Harry and Zo.

"What on … ?" muttered Harry.

"Chief Engineer Zo Harkman," said a familiar voice.

Admiral Achebe stepped through the security squad. Her face was stern, but her eyes wide, as though she couldn't quite believe what she was saying. "You're under arrest."

Zo gaped. "What for?"

"Evidence has come to light," said the Admiral. "Evidence that you …" She took a deep breath. "… sabotaged the power core."

"What?" Harry exploded. "He didn't – we just *fixed* it."

A pair of security guards shoved

him roughly to one side. One slipped
a glowing green cuff-loop around Zo's
wrists, while another took him by the

shoulder and steered
him towards the Mole.

"But this doesn't
make *sense*!" yelled
Harry. Anger was surging
through him now. How
could they think, for
one second, that his
guardian would do
anything to harm the
station? "It must be the
spy! Tell them, Zo."

The Admiral's gaze
fixed on Harry. She held up a hand.

"What did he just say? A *spy*?"

Harry stared at Zo. *Tell them*, he willed.

Zo hesitated, for just a moment …
then he shook his head. "I'm sorry,
Admiral. There's no spy. He's only trying
to help me." He turned to Harry, and his
eyes were glistening. "It'll be OK, Harry."

Harry watched, frozen in disbelief, as
the security guards marched Zo into the
Mole.

"To the brig," ordered Admiral Achebe,
and the Mole doors slid shut, leaving
Harry alone.

CHAPTER 4

TRAITOR

Harry took the Mole straight back up to the uppermost deck. He watched the deck numbers flickering past, clenching and unclenching his fists. *Come on, come on …* If the Admiral wouldn't listen, surely the Governor would see sense. She'd sort this out in no time.

As soon as Harry stepped back on to the Bridge, he was met by Secretary Bremmer, scowling as usual. "Stop right there, Cadet. You don't have the clearance to—"

"Please," burst out Harry, "I need to speak to the Governor." He could see her just beyond Bremmer, leaning over an Ob Tech's console.

Bremmer's jaw tightened. His eyes narrowed. "The Governor of Vantia1 doesn't have time to play games with children."

"I'm not *playing games*," Harry exploded. The anger was building inside him again. "They arrested Zo Harkman! He didn't do a thing wrong and—"

"Oh, didn't he?" Bremmer's eyebrows rose. "Perhaps you'd like to take a look at this, then?"

The Secretary grabbed Harry by the shoulder and marched him across the Bridge to an unattended console. With a few taps on the control pad, he brought up a 3D holographic video.

It took Harry a few moments to recognise the grainy image. It was security footage of the fernium blast door that led into the power core, time-stamped about forty-eight hours earlier. All was still. Then the door slid open.

Harry's stomach fell away. He felt dizzy. He had to lean on the console to steady himself.

There, clear as day, was Zo Harkman. He was dressed in one of the protective suits, but his face was unmistakeable through the visor. And in his hand …

"Power shears," said Bremmer, pointing. "The perfect tool for cutting cables, I'm sure you'll agree."

Harry nodded, in a daze. He wished with all his heart that Bremmer wasn't right – but he was.

The footage didn't show the power core itself. But a few moments later,

Harry saw Zo return and exit the way he'd come in. The blast door slid shut. The *clunk* as it locked seemed to end all of Harry's hopes.

Zo really *had* sabotaged the power core. He really was a traitor.

Harry couldn't believe what he had seen. It wasn't possible, was it? Not unless everything he knew about Zo Harkman was a lie.

The deck vibrated, and the whole station rumbled as the thrusters finally powered up. There were murmurs and sighs of relief all around.

"Station moving out of asteroid trajectory now," said A.D.U.R.O.

"Excellent work, everyone," said

Governor Knox. "Vantia1 is saved." Even she was smiling.

Harry hardly cared. He felt empty – hollowed out. Then his wrist computer bleeped with an alert. *30 minutes until the history test.*

As if today couldn't get any worse.

✪

Harry hurried down the corridors to the cadet classrooms, where the test was going to be held. He did his best to ignore the newsfeeds positioned throughout the station, but it seemed like there were screens at every corner. The rolling headlines taunted him.

SABOTAGE!

TREASON!

CHIEF ENGINEER BETRAYS VANTIA1!

The footage kept switching between the images Bremmer had shown him on the Bridge, and a video of Harkman being arrested, complete with Harry begging the Admiral to let him go.

His stomach felt as heavy as lead as he stepped into the test room.

Silence fell at once, and he felt a pair of eyes fixed on him from every desk.

"What's *he* doing here?" said Markus, as Harry sat beside Ava. The sneering cadet was leaning back on his chair at the back of the class, surrounded by his cronies. "He must have known what Harkman was up to. They should lock him up too."

For once, Harry didn't feel like fighting. But Ava spun round in her chair to snarl at Markus. "Shut it, space garbage. Like your mum would tell you a single thing about what she does all day."

Markus's face went bright red – with anger or embarrassment, Harry couldn't tell.

But then, luckily, the door slid open and Captain Nyman stepped in.

"Headsets on," he said briskly. "The

test will commence in thirty-four seconds."

"Are you OK?" whispered Ava, as the cadets began switching on their headsets.

"I'm fine," lied Harry. "It's all a misunderstanding. It'll get sorted out. I mean, I *know* Zo's not a criminal, so—"

"Harry Hugo," growled Captain Nyman. "Stop distracting Ava, if you please."

Harry pulled on his own headset, adjusted the band and lowered the visor. He thumbed the 'on' pad.

But as the first questions flashed across Harry's visor, he couldn't concentrate at all. If only he could talk to Zo ... Get him to explain what he was doing there, in the power core … with power shears … He frowned hard. Even he had to admit, it didn't look good.

"They'll probably send the pair of you to a penal colony," whispered Markus from behind. "Maybe a mining planet. I bet that robo-arm's great for breaking rocks, right?"

✪

Harry had flunked the test – no doubt about it. Not that he really cared right at that moment.

He slouched his way back to his quarters on Deck 5, guiltily taking the long way round to avoid Farooq and the other engineers, in case they were still working on that busted console.

But as he turned the corner, he froze. The door to his quarters was wide open, and a security guard was loitering outside.

Harry ducked back and waited until the guard was distracted, picking at his nails. Then he darted out, through the door and into the living room. "Hey!" called the guard from behind.

The place was full of station security. They were pulling open drawers, shredding sofa cushions, feeling along the edges of the vidscreens …

"What's going on?" Harry shouted.

A red-coated guard turned to him, the gold stripes of a corporal glinting on his sleeve. "Governor's orders," he grunted. He showed Harry his wrist device, and a warrant flashed up on the screen, with the Governor's signature clearly visible. "We're searching for evidence. You can wait outside."

Harry dashed instead to his own bedroom. There were three more guards in there. One of them was fiddling with the holograph of his family that hovered beside his bed. One was sorting through his clothes, while the third was taking a screwdriver to his Space Stallion.

"I wouldn't do that if I were you …" Harry warned.

Too late. Lights flickered across the Stallion, and a stream of hydraulic fluid shot out of a vent on its side. The guard stumbled back, spluttering. "Urgh! It's all over my uniform!"

"Best st-steer clear, part-part-partner," said the Stallion.

A heavy hand fell on Harry's shoulder, and he looked up into the corporal's glowering face. "You need to leave us, son. Unless you want to be arrested too?"

Harry was about to reply when every security guard's wrist screen flashed red.

"Emergency meeting," said the corporal. "All of you, with me."

"What now?" asked Harry, as the guards piled out of his bedroom.

"Not that it's any of your business, boy," said the Corporal, "but the asteroid's changed to a new course. A *collision* course."

CHAPTER 5

FIRESHIP

Harry stood alone in his empty quarters, surrounded by the wreckage of his and Zo Harkman's belongings. His mind was reeling. _A collision course ..._ But that wasn't possible, was it? Asteroids didn't just change course – they followed orbits, according to laws of gravity.

His wrist communicator bleeped. Then Ava's voice came crackling through. Harry heard the tension in it at once. "Harry! Have you heard? Apparently there's this asteroid, and it's … *following* us or something."

"I heard," said Harry. "What shall we do?"

"Come up to Deck 6."

Harry was out the door and halfway to the nearest Mole dock when the huge vidscreen at the end of the corridor went black. He felt a rush of relief as the image of his guardian being arrested disappeared. But a moment later, relief turned to worry. Governor Knox's face filled the screen, her brow fiercely knit.

"Attention, citizens of Vantia1," said the Governor. "Please remain calm. I am an initiating a station-wide evacuation order, with immediate effect. All citizens please report to the Flight Deck for transfer to Vantia2. I repeat, please remain—"

A thundering of feet drowned out the word "calm", as a family burst from their quarters and piled into the Mole. The two children were younger than Harry, and they just looked confused. But their parents were pale and wide-eyed.

So much for remaining calm.

Shouts and scuffling footsteps echoed throughout the deck. It sounded like a stampede … Harry darted to the Mole and slipped through the closing doors just in time.

A few moments later the doors opened on Deck 6, where Ava was already waiting.

"Come on! We've got to get to my mum."

All around them, the people of Vantia1 were panicking. A tall tattooed man barged Ava aside, hefting a creaking old space chest. Then a gang of teenagers hurtled past, running so fast that Harry had to flatten himself against the wall so as not to be knocked over.

"This isn't going to work," hissed Ava. "There aren't enough craft to evacuate the whole station. They'll have to send rescue vessels from Vantia2."

"And it's a two-hour journey to Vantia2," added Harry. "Best case, I reckon a quarter of us would make it."

He felt a sudden surge of desperation. If only Zo was here … Zo would stay calm. Zo would just treat it like a puzzle. Figure out what to do.

"There must be a way to save the station," said Harry.

"Yeah, right," said Ava. "I mean, all we need to do is stop ten thousand megatonnes of space ice hurtling towards us at—"

Harry gripped her arm. "The test," he said.

Ava stared at him. "Wait, you're

seriously worried about the *test*? We're about to be space dust and you're—"

"No! I mean, yes, but ..." Harry shook his head. "I need to talk to your mum. I've got an idea."

✪

"You again?" spluttered Secretary Bremmer, when they stepped on to the Bridge. He stopped halfway to Governor Knox and Admiral Achebe, who were holding a conversation by the command chair. "How did you—"

"Used my security pass," said Ava, holding it up and smiling sweetly. "Thirty seconds. Please, Mum. That's all he needs."

Harry held his breath. Everyone on

the bridge was staring at them now – Knox, Achebe … Not to mention every Ob Tech under the huge dome.

The Admiral glared at her daughter. "Thirty seconds," she said. "And not a moment more."

"Call off the evacuation," Harry burst out.

Governor Knox raised an eyebrow. "I beg your pardon?"

"We can stop the asteroid," said Harry. "We just need a fireship."

"What is the boy blathering about?" growled Bremmer.

Admiral Achebe's eyes were glinting. "Go on."

"I read about it for the history test," said Harry. "I mean, *in* the test. It was one of the questions. I didn't actually study for ... Well, that's not important." He felt his cheeks burning. "In naval battles, back on Avantia, sometimes a single ship was loaded up with gunpowder, or set on fire. Then it was sent straight into the enemy fleet. They called it a fireship."

"Nobody cares about your *history test*, boy," snapped Secretary Bremmer. "We have a crisis on our hands!"

"We could do the same thing," interrupted Harry. "Load a craft with high explosives. Send it straight into the asteroid. If it works, the asteroid would break up into fragments."

"Then the Moat would do the rest," added Ava. "Blow it all to smithereens."

There was a long silence. Harry held his breath. Everyone was looking at the Governor, who was frowning, deep in thought. "Admiral," she said at last. "Any ideas?"

"We'd need a space cruiser," said Ava's mum. "Titan class, at least. And it would have to be a shell, completely packed with explosives. Everything else inside – it would all need to be stripped

away." The smile spread across her face.
"But yes. It could work."

Harry's heart pounded, and adrenaline flooded his limbs. Ava squeezed his arm tight.

"About that stripping out," said Harry. "I've got just the team for the job."

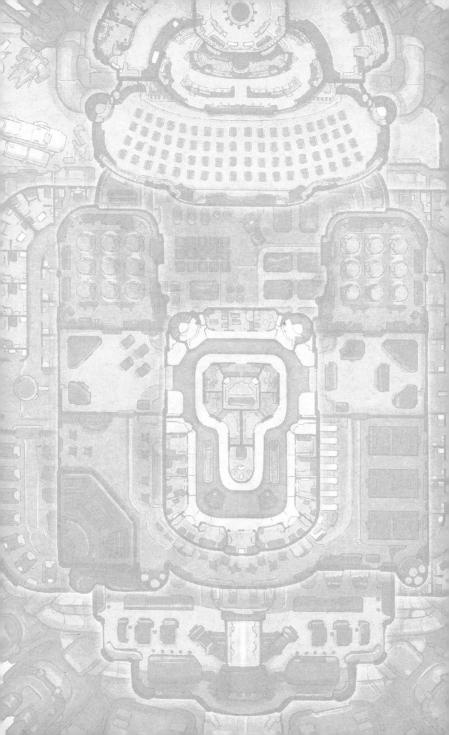

CHAPTER **6**

A SHADOWY FIGURE

Harry was hot and sweaty and his muscles ached from an hour's work with hydraulic cutters … but he couldn't wipe the grin off his face.

The space cruiser they'd chosen was monstrous, an old wreck in need of a new paint job, upgraded thrusters and a thousand other fixes. *Perfect for the fireship*. Harry was hard at work in the cockpit while engineers swarmed in and out like ants, ripping and cutting everything from the cargo lockers to the pilots' seats.

"So we all get promotions after this, right?" said Mei. Harry's old buddy from Engineering had partnered up with him to operate their cutter. The devices were so big and heavy, it was a two-person job. She flashed him a rare smile.

"You'll be lucky," said Harry, as they started on a disused guidance array. Sparks flew as the cutter bit deep. Harry wiped his brow with one hand.

In no time they were done, and unloaded the cutters. A couple of the bigger engineers – Farooq and Jackson – hefted the array and carted it out of the cruiser. At last it was finished. An empty shell. *Now for the dangerous part.*

As they headed out on to the flight deck, marines in dark green uniforms were already arriving with trolleys full of silver barrels. Each one was marked with a row of warning symbols.

Mei whistled. "Soltron-7! Better hope no one drops a barrel. The whole station will blow."

The grease-smeared crowd of engineers parted, shuffling back to the edges of the flight deck as the team of marines began loading the explosives on to the empty ship.

As it was happening, Governor Knox herself approached from the Mole with Admiral Achebe beside her. A hundred pairs of boots thumped on metal as everyone on the deck came to attention.

"Stand easy," barked the Admiral.

The pair of them inspected the ship, conferred a little, and the Governor gave a nod.

"Good work, team. There'll be bonus credits in this for all of you."

She didn't add "*if we survive*," but Harry knew she was thinking it.

"Cadet Hugo. You may join us on the Bridge if you like."

"Er … actually …" stammered Harry, "I'm good here, thanks."

Mei's eyebrows shot up.

Admiral Achebe simply shrugged. "Very well." She raised her voice so that the whole Flight Deck could hear. "Now stand by for launch."

✪

In a common room on the Engineering Deck, the engineers clustered around a huge wall-mounted vidscreen. Harry and Mei hovered at the back of the crowd. Everyone was muttering and shifting around uncomfortably, and Harry could feel the tension like electricity crackling through the room. There was only one question now.

Is this actually going to work?

"Thar she blows!" shouted someone, suddenly. Cheers and whoops rose up. Harry craned his neck and caught a glimpse of the screen. There was the ancient space cruiser, rocketing out of a

bay on the Flight Deck, thrusters firing white hot as it powered into space. It was being piloted remotely by A.D.U.R.O.

The room fell silent as the cruiser became a dot, then a speck, until it disappeared among the stars. Eyes switched to the screen showing the fireship's progress towards its target, complete with a timer counting down.

For the next few minutes, across the station, eyes were glued to the many screens showing the path of the fireship into space. Standing with the other engineers, Harry thought that it felt a bit like old times.

"I think it's going to work," muttered Mei.

"Yep," agreed Farooq. "They can have their fancy weapons and uniforms, but it's the engineers who saved the day."

But Harry had noticed something on the screen. The ship seemed to be veering slightly off-course.

His stomach churned. *Something's wrong.*

"What is it?" asked Mei.

But now it was obvious. The ship had steered way off its trajectory. It was going to miss its target. Across the room, the engineers began to stand, their faces alarmed.

Farooq shook his head in disbelief. "I thought that brainbox A.D.U.R.O. was in charge!"

"The remote transmitter," muttered Harry. "Has anyone checked the transmitter?" But nobody was listening.

Darting out of the door, Harry ran through the empty corridors of the Engineering Deck. What Farooq had said was true – A.D.U.R.O was indeed guiding the fireship, but Harry knew the signal was sent from a transmitter.

Rounding a corner, he reached the control room where the transmitter was located. He tapped in the access code and entered a narrow, dimly lit space lined with banks of humming, blinking modules twice his height. There was the transmitter console, right at the end.

He was halfway there when he heard a *CLUNK*, and the lights died.

Harry froze. *What on … ?*

Some kind of power failure, obviously.

Maybe that was the problem with the transmitter.

All the same, a chill crept down his spine. Feeling across his prosthetic arm, Harry activated the built-in torch. It shone a cold white light up ahead, and he hurried to the transmitter.

As his eyes darted across the controls, he saw it wasn't a power failure at all. The transmitter had been switched off – disabled manually.

Sabotage – again?

His fingers danced across the controls. In moments, green lights glowed across the console, and it was back online.

He was about to heave a sigh of relief when he heard the soft squeak of a boot, somewhere behind him.

He spun, holding out his prosthetic arm. The torch beam slid across the stacks of consoles …

Nothing. No one to be seen.

Fffffzzapp! A blaster bolt seared past in a flash of red, so close Harry felt its heat on his cheek. He flung himself to one side, heart pounding. *That was close.* It had come from near the doorway. And he was about to shine his torch there, when he heard the hum of the blaster powering up for another shot …

He twisted and threw his prosthetic arm across his body like a shield.

Fffffzzzzapp! His arm jolted, smacking him in the face and knocking him off

balance. He stumbled and fell. His nose hurt. There was blood on his face; a smell of burning.

His arm was smoking. Its exposed struts were half melted and twisted out of shape. Circuits sparked and sizzled. *I've been hit ...*

Out of the corner of his eye, he saw the door slide open, light spilling in.

"Hey! Stop!" he shouted.

Harry glanced round, spotted a spanner and snatched it up. He rerouted power to his prosthetic arm and hurled the tool as fast as he could at the figure.

CLANG! The spanner left a dent in the wall opposite, but the stranger had already gone.

Harry went in pursuit, pumping his legs for all he was worth. As he turned the corner, he saw a boot disappearing through a heavy blast door. *Uh oh.* He ran faster, hurtling down the corridor. He could hear frantic tapping at the keypad beyond the door. A lock code.

THUNK!

The door slammed shut, and Harry smacked straight into it.

He slid to the floor, panting. The chase was over.

INVINCIBLE

"Do you see?" Harry brandished his arm, displaying the mess of broken circuits and scorched metal. He was back on the Bridge, escorted this time by two security personnel.

Secretary Bremmer sighed loudly. "See what, exactly?"

"Zo Harkman is innocent!" Harry couldn't help raising his voice. "He *has* to be. He's locked up in the brig, so he couldn't have sabotaged the transmitter. And he definitely couldn't have shot me in the arm. The person I was chasing – whoever they are, it's them who's responsible. They're probably working for Vellis. And they tried to kill me!"

Admiral Achebe and Governor Knox shared a glance. Harry knew he was getting through.

"Do you have any proof?" said the Governor.

Harry gestured helplessly with his damaged arm. "Here's the proof! And ... and there must be security footage."

Admiral Achebe cleared her throat. "I'm afraid we've already tried that. It seems there was an error."

"It's Vellis's agent!" cried Harry. "They've covered their tracks."

But the Governor and the Admiral were stony-faced.

"I'm sorry, Cadet," said Governor Knox. "Once we've dealt with the current crisis, you have my word that we'll look into this."

Harry's shoulders slumped. He was beaten. There was nothing more he could say.

"Look!" squawked Bremmer suddenly. He was pointing at an Ob Tech's console. "The fireship is nearing the target."

"Patch it to the main screen," ordered the Admiral.

The vidscreen filled with an image from the space cruiser's cameras as it soared through space. *Back on course.* Beyond it, Harry saw something that took his breath away. The asteroid – a shimmering, blue-white boulder of ice. Gigantic. Doubt flashed through his mind. *Will the explosives be enough?*

"Impact in 10 seconds," said A.D.U.R.O. Quiet fell across the Bridge. Everyone stared at the screen as the AI counted down: "3 ... 2 ... 1 ..."

The fireship was a tiny black speck against the impossibly vast asteroid. Then the image went blank.

"Did it work?" asked Bremmer.

A.D.U.R.O. spoke calmly. "My sensors indicate the asteroid was destroyed."

Harry could hardly believe it, but a second later the station rumbled beneath their feet as the blast wave hit.

"We did it!" said Knox. "Well done, everyone!"

Suddenly everyone was on their feet, punching the air, embracing and laughing. Harry even forgot for a moment that Zo Harkman was still locked up in the brig. Admiral Achebe was watching Harry. She wasn't quite smiling, but her eyes sparkled, and she gave him a firm nod.

"Erm … we have another problem," said one of the Ob Techs.

"What now?" said Governor Knox.

The Ob Tech was pushing controls on his panel. "Something is happening to the asteroid fragments … A.D.U.R.O, can you provide a visual?"

The main screen flickered and a blurred image appeared. This one showed the aftermath of the explosion, with the shattered chunks of the asteroid. But something wasn't right at all. Instead of shooting off into space, the pieces of rock were *curling* back inwards.

Straight towards Vantia1 ...

"Impossible," breathed Admiral Achebe. "They're like heat-seeking missiles!"

Harry swallowed hard. It didn't make any sense. Lumps of rock didn't behave like missiles. They didn't have thrusters. They should behave according to the laws of physics.

But suddenly he understood. They *were* obeying the laws of physics.

"Something's *pulling* them!" he cried.

"This boy is insufferable," muttered Bremmer.

But the Governor held up a hand. "What do you mean?"

"We need to activate short-range scanners," said Harry breathlessly. "There must be something generating gravitational force, somewhere on the station – or nearby."

The Admiral shook her head. "Harry, it would have to be something *huge* to—"

"Do it," interrupted the Governor.

"Scanning," said the calm voice of A.D.U.R.O. Then she spoke again. "Source found."

The Admiral's eyebrows shot up. "What?"

"Object located off starboard hull," said A.D.U.R.O. "Displaying now."

The vidscreen switched to a new view. The edge of the station's hull curved away at one side of the screen. Next to it, there was only the darkness of space. "Applying graviton-scan overlay," said A.D.U.R.O.

A shimmering filter slid across the screen. And the Bridge fell silent once again.

"What *is* that?" squeaked Bremmer. "It looks like ..."

"A squid," said Harry, feeling dizzy with horror. "A giant squid."

The creature was glistening silver in the overlay. Its mantle was the size of a battle cruiser itself, the edges waving gently up and down like seaweed underwater. Ten tentacles dangled beneath, lazily drifting in the darkness. It was enormous. And all this time it had been floating, invisible, right next to the station.

No one on Vantia1 had any idea!

"It's Vellis," croaked Harry. "It has to be another one of his monsters."

"What are we looking at, A.D.U.R.O.?" said Admiral Achebe grimly.

"High concentrations of gravitons," said A.D.U.R.O. "Localised and focused."

"That *thing* is sending out bursts of gravitational waves, Governor," said an Ob Tech. "Enough to pull the asteroid fragments in towards the station."

The Governor had gone very pale.

But now she turned to Admiral Achebe and gave her the nod.

"Scramble a squadron of Barracudas," barked Achebe. "Neutralise that ... *whatever* it is."

As Ob Techs relayed the orders down to the Flight Deck, Harry shifted on his feet. He had a sick feeling in his stomach. He remembered how deadly the robo-dragon had proved. Vellis was cunning and without pity.

"Admiral?" He spoke in a low voice. "Don't you think Vellis might be expecting an attack?"

Achebe frowned. "What do you suggest?"

"If we run some more scans ..."

"We don't have time for that!" scoffed Bremmer. "Need I remind you all about the giant asteroid hurtling towards us? Or rather, the thousand slightly smaller asteroids, thanks to this genius boy!"

Harry clenched his fists with anger, but the Governor waved a hand. "Secretary Bremmer is right. Let's blast this squid apart, and quickly."

"Engage," ordered Admiral Achebe.

Three squat, heavy grey gunships emerged from a bay on-screen and cruised towards the squid. The Barracudas weren't fast, but Harry knew they carried the most powerful blaster cannons that Zo's engineers could build.

The gunships fanned out, encircling the squid. The monster's tentacles drifted gently. It didn't even try to escape.

The queasy feeling grew stronger in the pit of Harry's stomach.

"Awaiting your orders," said a pilot over the intercom.

"Give it all you've got," said Achebe quietly.

Light flared across the screen, so bright that Harry had to squint and shield his eyes with a hand. The Barracudas had opened fire, pelting the squid with high-energy blasts, bombs and slicer missiles. *It's like a fireworks display ...*

But as his eyes adjusted to the flashes of the weaponry, Harry gasped.

The squid was changing colour. With every impact its body turned silver and gold. Almost as though it was absorbing the energy of the attack. Its tentacles stretched and flexed.

"Come in, Vantia1!" The pilot's voice sounded panicked now. "Our systems are going haywire, I don't … I don't understand!"

"Pull out!" cried Achebe. "Pull out now!"

But it was too late.

The cannons ceased fire. The screen grew dark. The ships hung in space, motionless. *Like flies caught in a spider's web*, thought Harry.

"What's happening?" said the pilot.

Then the squid's body spasmed, lighting up like a glow-worm. A shudder ran right through it, and the ships hurtled away, spinning through space at impossible speed.

Harry spotted the pilots ejecting, escape pods streaking silver ... Then more flashes seared across the screen, as the Barracudas smashed into smithereens against the hull of Vantia1.

"What *was* that?" asked Governor Knox, in the silence which followed.

Harry frowned. So Vellis had designed the squid with a powerful defence mechanism ... But it had been slow to react. *Could it be ... Perhaps the squid didn't detect the Barracudas until they opened fire?*

His thoughts were interrupted as the Admiral strode to the console with a face like thunder. "Enough!" she growled. "Activate the Moat guns. Tear it apart!"

The external cannons swung into life, swivelling and locking on the squid. Rapid-fire blaster bolts scorched across the screen like angry hornets.

At last the squid squirmed into life. With a pulse of its tentacles, it cruised in

past the blaster fire and twisted in mid-space. A cloud emerged from among the tentacles, black and noxious, like a burst of ink. As the shroud of gas settled across the Moat guns, the cannons stopped firing.

"Malfunction on the gun turrets," reported an Ob Tech. "Make that malfunctions. Multiple malfunctions."

"You've made your point," snapped Achebe. She ran a hand furiously across her close-cropped head. "Any ideas? Anyone? How do we beat this space vermin?"

"It's invincible," said Bremmer, wide-eyed.

"*Nothing's* invincible," said Harry. "It's a robot, just like the dragon was. That means it's controlled by a system. And systems have weaknesses. If we can just find the squid's ..."

"What are you saying, Cadet?" asked the Admiral.

Harry stared at his arm. Slowly, an idea was forming in his mind.

"Hugo!" barked the Admiral, again.

But Harry didn't reply. Instead he darted towards the Mole, heart racing.

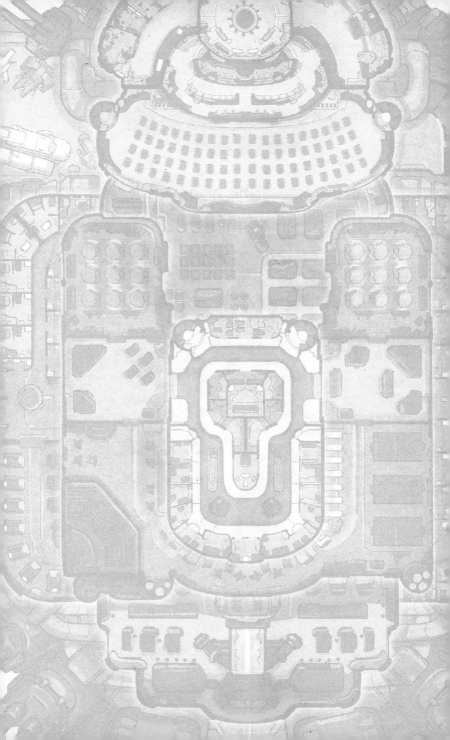

CHAPTER 8

HERE GOES NOTHING

Ava was already waiting for him when the doors slid open on the Flight Deck. Harry had buzzed her from the Mole. "What now?" she asked, raising an eyebrow.

"You'll see." Harry barrelled past her,

waving for her to follow.

Across the deck, a cluster of engineers were working on the landing gear of a transport vessel, while a group of anxious evacuees hovered nearby, loaded with luggage and desperate to get their flight out of Vantia1. But one of the officials was on the boarding ramp, shaking his head. "I've had orders from up top – no one else is leaving," he yelled. "There's something out there."

That set off a chorus of panic among the crowd. "But one ship has already left!" someone shouted.

"Mei!" called Harry, spotting his old buddy.

Mei slid out from under the landing

gear and holstered her wrench. "Bit busy, Hazza."

"It'll only take a minute." Harry held out his robotic arm. "I need you to fix me up with a hydraulic cutter."

"Do *what*?"

"Attach it to my arm."

"Are you sure?" said Ava, doubtfully.

As the official tried to calm the panicking civilians, Mei stood up, took Harry's arm and examined it like a doctor about to perform surgery. A slow smile spread across her face. "Always wanted to have a tinker with this thing."

There was a welding station not far from the vessel. Mei got to work right away, while two other engineers held the massive hydraulic cutter in position. Ava stood to one side, looking more puzzled all the time.

Sparks flew, and Harry felt the heat of the work travelling up his arm. He gritted his teeth. But in minutes Mei flipped up her visor and grinned. "Congratulations, Hazza," she said. "You're a human can opener."

Harry tried to move his arm. *Clunk!* It dragged him down to the deck. *Whoa – it's even heavier than I thought* ... He quickly rerouted power from secondary functions, boosting his synthetic muscles so that he could actually lift the cutter. He tested the circuits, and the cutter whirred briefly into life. *Nice!*

"I owe you one," he told Mei.

"Out of the way!"

Harry looked up at the familiar voice. Markus was shoving his way through the throng of people who were waiting to board the evacuation transport. He'd removed his uniform and wore casual clothes. Harry saw a little girl stumble as Markus barged past. She couldn't have been more than five years old.

"Hey!" he shouted. "What are you doing?"

Markus froze. "Making sure everyone gets on board safely, obviously."

"Really?" said Ava, hands on hips. "What's with the case, then?"

Harry saw that Markus was holding a

bulging holdall in one hand.

What a coward! thought Harry.

"Maybe you haven't heard," he said. "The evacuation's off."

"You're stuck here like the rest of us," added Ava.

Markus's cheeks flushed. "We'll see about that!" he said, storming off towards the official.

A commotion behind made Harry turn. Engineers were ducking and dodging out of the way as a gleaming red vehicle shot out of the Mole and *whooshed* to a halt at Harry's side.

"How-how-howdy," said the Space Stallion.

Harry grinned. He'd almost forgotten

that he'd issued a summon command to the Stallion on the way down here.

I've really got to sort out that new voice chip ...

"Pretty sure that thing's not allowed down here," said Mei, frowning.

"So long as no one tells," said Harry with a grin. He leapt up into the saddle and thumbed a button on his belt, and his space-skin activated, covering his body and head like a clear second skin.

"Harry!" Ava's eyes had gone wide. "I hope you're not planning what I think you're planning."

"You can't go out there!" said Mei.

Harry's eyes darted to the launch bays, which were closed. A squad of security officers were stationed there. They'd spotted him, and were already muttering into their communicators.

If I can pass them, I'm home free ...

"Ava, can you get the doors, please?" he said.

"Harry, I don't think ..."

Harry twisted the throttle. The Stallion's thrusters roared, and his stomach lurched as they shot across the Flight Deck. The security team drew their blasters and pointed them towards him.

"Stop right there!" one said. Harry jerked at the handlebars, swerving to a halt. The Stallion hummed. The officer strode towards him. "No unauthorised access to space."

Out of the corner of his eye, Harry saw that Ava had edged closer to one of the consoles by another launch bay. She caught his eye. She looked anxious, but she gave him a firm nod.

He twisted the throttle again, as far as it would go. The Stallion roared straight past the security guards, so close they stumbled away in shock.

"Sorry!" Harry called over his shoulder.

Then Ava tapped the console, and the launch bay door slid open in front of him. He kept going, straight through the airlock, not slowing for an instant. *Whooosh.* The airlock doors hissed open too, and Harry zoomed out into the blackness of space.

Wheeling round, he spotted the
first transport, already listing badly. Its
thrusters were white-hot, firing full blast,
but it was hardly moving forwards. Then
he saw why. Beyond it was the Gravity
Squid, its body pulsating.

Harry's breath caught in his throat.
Up close it was even bigger than he'd
imagined. It was completely visible
now, as though it was no longer
bothering to camouflage itself. Its
body was shimmering silver and gold
and quivering, tentacles flicking and
spasming as it worked its gravitational
power on the transport vessel.

It's distracted ...

Harry knew he might never get a

better chance. He gunned the engines and raced towards the squid, trying to ignore his pounding heart. He activated the cutter, the blades whirring into life.

Here goes nothing.

Harry swept past the nearest tentacle and sliced at it. The blade sank in deep, and Harry nearly fell off his Stallion. Just in time, he got the blade free and hauled himself back into his saddle.

The squid's tentacles twisted and lashed, and Harry knew it had felt the cutter, in whatever passed for its brain.

The monster spun slowly. And suddenly the tentacles were moving fast – faster than Harry had thought possible. They whipped towards him, flickering through space …

Harry jinked and dodged, crouching low and gripping tight to the Stallion with his knees. Out of the corner of his eye, he saw the transport jerk suddenly away, as the squid's gravitational attack gave out. The vessel powered through space, free from the monster. *Saved*.

Harry's heart lifted. He twisted the throttle, weaving faster, in and out of the flailing tentacles. He swiped with his cutter arm again, and felt the drag as the blade bit deep once more. This time the glistening end of the tentacle went spiralling off into space, severed entirely.

I'm winning!

Swerving round for another attack,

Harry swung his arm as hard as he could. He felt the *thump* as the cutter sliced into yet another tentacle …

But this time, the blade stuck fast.

The Stallion kept surging forward, and Harry couldn't hold on. The handlebars were torn from his grasp, and he stared in horror as the Stallion shot away from him, riderless.

Harry felt cold all over.

He'd got cocky. He'd struck the monster too hard.

He shut down all power to the cutter. Desperately he tried to prise it free from the squid's flesh. But it was lodged deep.

Now the squid was lifting him up, helpless. A pair of huge, mirrored sensors on its mantle swivelled like eyes to observe him.

And with a jolt of horror, Harry saw something at the very centre of the squid, where the tentacles emerged from its mantle. A gaping, shining black beak, curved into two razor-sharp points.

The tentacle carried him towards the squid's mouth.

CHAPTER 9

A MONSTER'S HEART

Harry routed every last unit of power into his synthetic muscles. He hauled at his arm, straining his whole body.

At last it came free, and he floated off. Almost immediately another tentacle bashed into him, sending him spinning. He crashed ribs-first into the creature's mantle. Its flesh was soft, coated with some sort of rubbery material, but he felt mechanical workings beneath. The squid lurched and shuddered, trying to throw him off.

Harry gritted his teeth. *I don't think so.*

He clawed his way along, past the eye-like sensors. Up ahead he could see the outline of a silver circle embedded in the squid's flesh, and his heart leapt. *A service hatch!*

All systems have a weakness, he thought, with a grim smile.

The hatch slid smoothly open, and Harry crawled through.

He was *inside* the squid.

Looking around, he saw that he was at an intersection of narrow metal corridors, only just high enough for him to float upright. But as the hatch closed, artificial gravity kicked in and his boots thumped to the ground. He set out, stumbling along the passageway.

The walls weren't quite what he'd thought. They were curved, and ribbed, like the insides of a creature's intestines. Like the outer coating of the squid, they were made of material slightly slimy, and yielding to the touch. Every few moments the gleaming surfaces rippled with lights, like the pulse of a heartbeat.

The corridor sloped and curled rather

than following a straight line, seeming to narrow and widen again, flexing like a living thing as he made his way. Here and there other tunnels branched off to the sides, leading into darkness. Harry's stomach churned with claustrophobia. *What am I doing here?*

If he could find some kind of control system, maybe there was a chance he could disarm the squid. On the other hand, maybe he was just going further and further into danger. Maybe he'd get lost in here and wander around until he eventually grew too weak ... and then simply die.

He followed the path of the flashing lights, but in reverse. His theory was that the source might well be the core of Vellis's creation. It turned out to be right, because quite suddenly he rounded a corner and came upon a large, circular chamber. Harry gasped.

In the centre was a glowing orb of light, about twice the size of his Space Stallion. It was pulsing too, and it hung from the walls of the chamber on twisting branches of light.

Harry could tell at once that it was a gravitational engine – the one that generated the squid's incredible powers. It looked more than a little like a gigantic, beating heart.

A shiver ran down his spine.

Harry's every instinct screamed at him

to turn and run. But he'd come this far. And if he could disconnect the squid's heart from its body …

Peering closer at the branches of light, Harry saw that they were actually brightly glowing cables. He tugged gently at one, but it stayed attached. Holding his breath, Harry gripped a cable, hauled himself up, and began to shin along it. He had to squint through the brightness as he reached the central core. But between the pulses of light, he saw that the surface of the core was covered in circuitry and control panels.

His heart beat faster. The squid might look completely alien, but there was nothing alien about the control panels. A few tweaks here and there, and he could overload the system. Then stabilising protocols would kick in and shut the whole thing down.

He smiled. Two could play at sabotage.

Of course, if I'm wrong, the gravitational forces might just rip me apart like wet cardboard.

Harry's hand hovered over the circuitry …

"I wouldn't do that, if I were you," said a voice from below.

Harry looked down.

There, standing by the entrance to the chamber, was a figure he recognised at once. A pale man with a short beard and a bald head. He wore a close-fitting black

suit, and he was smiling up at Harry, his
dark eyes glittering with amusement.

"Vellis," Harry
whispered.

"You can't
win," said Vellis.
"Give up now, is
my advice. You
don't want to miss
my little monster
destroying Vantia1
now, do you?"

Harry bit his lip. Vellis wasn't armed.
And this might be the only chance he got.

He swung his leg over the cable and
dropped to the chamber floor. At the
same time, he activated the cutter on his

arm. It roared into life, deafeningly loud in the echoing chamber.

Vellis did nothing. Just watched, still smiling. Even as Harry swung the cutter ...

Whooosh. The blade passed right through the scientist, as though he wasn't there at all.

Vellis's whole body flickered. Then it was gone entirely.

Harry's gaze darted to the floor, where a metallic green sphere, no bigger than a marble, rolled gently to a stop against the chamber wall. *A holographic projector,* Harry realised, flushing.

"Bravo, Harry," said Vellis's voice, from the projector.

"I should've known you'd be too

cowardly to show yourself," Harry snapped back.

"Says the boy who just struck an unarmed man," taunted Vellis. "I only wish I could be here in person to see—"

Harry stamped down hard on the projector, crunching it beneath his boot.

There was no time to lose. Vellis must have been trying to stop him from messing with the gravitational engine. *Which means I'm on the right track.*

Harry quickly hauled himself back on to the cable and returned to the core. This time he didn't hesitate. He tapped at a control panel, tugged a circuit board loose. He let it clatter to the ground. The pulses of light suddenly sped up. As

though the squid's heart was beating
faster.

Getting somewhere ...

He pulled out another, then jammed
his cutting blade inside.

Suddenly, the whole chamber shook
and rumbled, and Harry lost his balance,
tumbling to the deck below. Glancing
back, he saw the lights flickering, flashing
in a random pattern now.

"That should do it," he muttered.

Harry's own heart was racing as he
darted for the exit. But something was
wrong. His legs were heavy, as though
they were made of lead. Out of the
chamber and back in the corridor, it felt
like an invisible hand was pulling him

back. And with a lurch of his stomach he realised … it was! Somehow the gravitational force of the engine was acting inside the squid's body.

Terror spiked in Harry's chest. He had to get out of there.

Reaching out with his robotic arm, he seized hold of the edge of the corridor. Then he worked his synth muscles for all they were worth. Gradually, he pulled himself out of the chamber.

The force was getting stronger every moment. Harry fought against it, trying to remember the way back to the service hatch. It was like wading through treacle that got thicker every second.

The lights were flashing wildly on

and off now. The walls and floor of the corridor trembled, then shook, almost knocking Harry off his feet.

There – the service hatch, up ahead.

Harry activated his space-skin, then slammed his robotic arm up hard into the hatch. The door came away at once, spiralling off into space. And Harry pulled himself up and out of the squid, gasping with relief.

Crouching on the soft jelly-like mantle, he thumbed a codepad on his forearm to summon his Stallion. There it was, soaring out of the darkness. Harry reached for it, muscles trembling with the effort, and got one hand tight to the handlebars. He twisted the throttle and let the Stallion haul him away. He just wanted to put as much distance as he could between himself and the squid.

But it wasn't enough. Even though the Stallion's thrusters were at maximum, it was slowing down, powerless against the growing gravitational pull.

Over his shoulder, Harry could see the squid's tentacles thrashing and spasming with distress. *No wonder.* Its heart was collapsing. And if he wasn't careful, the gravitational forces would take him down with it ... The Stallion's controls were flashing warnings about an overload. They began to go backwards. His own grip was loosening on the handlebars.

There was nothing he could do.

Glancing back, he saw that the tentacles were coiling and smashing into each other. Cracks were spreading across the surface of the squid, and parts of it were already breaking off and drifting free like space flotsam.

It was coming apart.

And at the same time, it was dragging Harry to his death.

CHAPTER 10

THE FERNIUM RING

Harry fought down the despair that threatened to overwhelm him. There had to be something he could do … some way out of this …

But the collapsing gravity engine was sucking him in. He crouched down low, twisting the throttle uselessly.

He was just a leaf caught in a hurricane.

Then a blue glow shone all around, glinting purple off the red panels of his Space Stallion. A cadet vessel was approaching – one of the old, beaten-up ones that Captain Nyman used for training. The blue glow came from its tractor beam, arcing through space and holding Harry and his Stallion in its grip.

He could still feel himself slipping backwards, though, towards the squid …

Then he noticed another training vessel, and a third, moving into position. Their tractor beams activated, hitting Harry like blue spotlights.

And now, at last, he was moving away from the dying squid. He let out a long, shaky breath. *Safe. I'm really safe …*

He glanced back once over his shoulder. Just long enough to see the squid's tentacles swirl away into nothingness, like the debris of a shattered asteroid. Long enough to see its mantle cave in entirely, becoming a silvery cloud of particles which shimmered away too.

Harry blinked. Vellis's giant squid was simply gone. Vanished into the black emptiness of space.

✪

As the tractor hatch closed behind Harry, he felt suddenly exhausted. All the adrenaline had drained out of him, and he slumped off his Space Stallion and on to the deck.

Applause sounded all around, startling him. He looked up to see the cadets all cheering and clapping. His cheeks burned with embarrassment.

"Not bad," said Ava, offering Harry her hand. The sight of her face brought a smile to his lips, and he stood, leaning heavily on her.

"Setting a course back to Vantia1," called the pilot from the cockpit. "Strap in."

As the cadets settled in crash seats at the edges of the craft, Ava helped Harry to the cockpit. "Sit up front," she told him. "I think you've earned it."

"Incoming transmission," said the pilot, as Harry and Ava buckled up just behind him.

A vidscreen flashed on, showing Governor Knox on the Bridge, with Secretary Bremmer at her side.

Harry held his breath. He couldn't quite read the Governor's expression. She looked half relieved and half angry.

"Cadet Hugo …" said Governor Knox. "That was out of line. And incredibly dangerous. And, well … very brave." Her lips twitched at the corners. "The asteroid fragments have been repelled, and we have recalled the evacuation vessels."

Harry gasped with relief. *We did it!*

"Vantia1 is safe," said the Governor. "Well done, Harry. Zo Harkman would be proud."

"Release him then," said Harry, before he could stop himself. "He's not a traitor. You *know* he's not."

Governor Knox hesitated. Harry could see the indecision written on her face.

Bremmer held up a hand to protest. "Governor, I applaud Cadet Hugo's actions as much as anyone, but none of this is proof that Zo Harkman is not in league with Vellis. We gave the security footage ..."

As he spoke, Harry noticed something on the screen. He jerked back. "No ..."

"What's wrong?" asked Ava. "Harry, you've gone white."

Harry shook himself and addressed the vidscreen. "Secretary Bremmer. Where did you get that ring?"

Governor Knox frowned in confusion.

"What?" said Ava.

Bremmer whipped his hand back behind his back. His eyes had gone wide. "What, er … What ring?"

But it was too late. Harry had seen it – the large, dull fernium ring that Bremmer wore on his forefinger. And set on top of it, like a gemstone, was a metallic green sphere. A sphere that Harry recognised.

"It's a holographic projector, isn't it?"

said Harry. "Just like the one Vellis uses."
He tried to stand, but the seatbelt held
him back. "It's you! You're the spy."

"I ... I don't ..." stammered Bremmer.
He gawped like a fish.

Governor Knox was staring at the

Secretary now.
She took a step
away from him.
"Bremmer ..." she
began.

But before she
could say anything
more, Bremmer
whipped out a
blaster. He levelled
it at the Governor.

Sweat stood out on his brow.

Gasps rose up from those on board the cadet vessel.

Harry gripped on tight to the armrests of his seat. "Wait!" he yelled. "Please, just—"

Then the screen went dead.

"Transmission ended," said a smooth, robotic voice.

CHAPTER 11

INTO THE VOID

The cadet vessel's landing ramp had barely lowered before Harry came roaring down it on his Space Stallion. Ava rode behind, clinging on tightly to his waist.

As they darted across the flight deck, Harry's heart was pounding. He didn't know how much time they had. *Maybe it's already too late ...*

"A.D.U.R.O., locate Governor Knox," he said. They tore up a curving access ramp towards the higher levels of the station.

The AI's calm face shimmered into view, hovering in miniature above the Stallion's handlebars. "Cadet Hugo, you do not have authority to—"

"Where is she?" snapped Ava. "Authorisation code 6K-7.92." She lowered her voice. "My mum's," she told Harry.

"Authorised," said A.D.U.R.O. "Governor Knox is in EEP bay Alpha."

The emergency escape pods! Harry's mouth went dry.

"Locate Secretary Bremmer," said Ava.

"Secretary Bremmer is in EEP bay Alpha," said A.D.U.R.O.

"He's taken her hostage," said Harry, as A.D.U.R.O.'s face shimmered away again. He jerked the handlebars, swerving down a corridor towards the EEP bays. "He's going to take her back to Vellis ..."

"I'll tell Mum." Ava tapped at her communicator and muttered into it, her words drowned out by the roar of the Stallion's thrusters.

Harry twisted the throttle, speeding up another ramp and round a corner. Then he hit the brakes, jolting them to a stop by a heavy sliding metal door framed by yellow and black emergency stripes. *EEP bay Alpha.*

The Stallion hummed, ticking over, as Harry leaned down from the saddle to hit the access pad. It flashed red.

"Locked." He slammed a fist on the handlebars in frustration. "What now?"

Ava shook her head grimly. "Even A.D.U.R.O. can't override the EEP bay locks."

"Then we've only got one choice." Harry flicked the Stallion into reverse, manoeuvering slowly round to face the doors head on.

"Whoa," said Ava. "Please tell me you're not going to use us as a battering ram?"

"Not exactly." Harry flipped a cover on

a large red button. "Always wanted to test these out."

At the push of the button, twin cannons slid from the Stallion's chassis.

"Not strictly within regulations," he said, then pulled the trigger.

Fffffzzzaaap!
Fffffzzzaaap!
Harry felt the heat searing through the bike as two red energy bolts slammed into the bay doors.

There was a groan and

a squeal of buckling metal, and smoke filled the hallway. As it slowly cleared, Harry could see the bay doors had gone. "Bullseye," he muttered. Then he gunned the thrusters and tore through.

There was a bank of ten to twenty pods opposite, stacked in two rows like the washing machines in a laundrette that Harry had seen in one of Zo Harkman's ancient movies.

"There!" Ava pointed frantically.

Harry spotted Secretary Bremmer at the end of the bay, frozen in the middle of tapping access codes into one of the pods with one hand. His other hand held the blaster, levelled straight at Governor Knox's head.

Bremmer and Knox stared at them.

"Stay back, both of you," said the Governor calmly. Her voice betrayed no fear, but her face was pale.

"You heard the Governor," said Bremmer, scowling. "You've done enough meddling, Cadet."

Anger surged through Harry. "*You're* the meddler," he snapped. "You've been a traitor all along."

Bremmer sneered. "Oh really? It was Zo Harkman who sabotaged the power core, remember?"

Harry shook his head. "I didn't understand it before. But now I've seen Vellis's hologram tech up close, I get it. It's way ahead of anything we can do on

Vantia1. You used a hologram of Zo to frame him, didn't you? Vellis must have made it for you."

Bremmer's sneer grew wider. He reached inside his jacket, and his appearance flickered. Suddenly Harry was looking at Harkman's familiar features. A moment later the image of Harkman was gone. "Congratulations," said Bremmer. "You figured it out. But it won't do you any good."

"I don't understand," said Ava, frowning. "Why are you doing this, Bremmer? Vellis is *evil*."

Bremmer snorted. "That's just another word for ambitious ... and powerful. You can't defeat him. He will reward his friends. And any who stand against him will be crushed like—"

Governor Knox drove her elbow hard into his ribs. Bremmer gasped, dropped the blaster and doubled up, clutching at his gut. Before he could recover, the Governor kicked the blaster, sending it skidding across the floor.

Quick as a flash, Ava dismounted from the Stallion and grabbed the weapon, aiming it at Bremmer. "Game over, Secretary," she said.

Bremmer smiled. "You wouldn't shoot an unarmed man," he said, backing into the pod.

Ava's hands were trembling.

"Do it!" shouted Governor Knox.

But it was too late. Bremmer tapped at the pod controls, and the pod door slid closed.

"Launch in 3," said an automated voice.

"No!" shouted Harry.

"2 ... 1 ..."

Harry reached the pod and banged his fists against the plexiglass. Bremmer just grinned at him from inside. *Goodbye, Cadet*, he mouthed.

Then with a hiss and a roar, the pod was gone, catapulted out into space in a blur of speed.

Harry, Ava and Governor Knox stared silently at the empty pod capsule.

Then there was a screech of metal,

as security officers dragged the half-melted doors apart, and Admiral Achebe clambered into the room. "Where is he?"

Harry pointed through a small viewing window at the pod, streaking away like a comet.

Achebe's jaw tightened. "A.D.U.R.O.! Activate tractor beams: target pod Alpha-19."

"Tractor beams offline," said A.D.U.R.O.'s voice, echoing through the bay.

"Bremmer's work," muttered Governor Knox, as she rose to her feet.

Ava was frowning. "Is he mad? He's heading straight for the Void."

Sure enough, Harry saw that the pod

was changing course, tacking towards the gigantic, whirling storm of light in the distance.

"But he'll die in there," said Admiral Achebe.

And then the truth dawned on Harry. "No, he won't." His skin prickled. "There's something Zo was working on. A special material he had, in a secret lab … It makes it possible to survive the Void."

Achebe's jaw dropped. Governor Knox's eyes widened.

"Bremmer must have stolen it," said Harry. "He probably stashed it in the escape pod, in case he needed it. He's going into the Void *on purpose*. He's going to join Vellis."

Silence fell once again. They all watched, through the viewing window, as the pod became a silver dot. Then a glimmer. Then it disappeared into the vast, swirling maelstrom of the Void.

"I'm sorry, Harry," said Ava, her eyes downcast. "I should've stopped him, but he was right – I couldn't take the shot. Not when he wasn't even armed."

"Don't beat yourself up," said Harry. "That's what separates us from them."

✪

Clunk. The locking mechanism deactivated, and the reinforced door of the cell slid open.

In the small, darkened room, Harry saw a familiar face turn to him.

"Zo!" he gasped. Tears pricked at his eyes. Then he was running, and his guardian swept him up in a bear hug so tight that Harry thought Zo might break every bone in his body. He didn't care, though.

"Chief Engineer Harkman, you are free to go," said Admiral Achebe, stiffly, when they broke apart at last. "And … we all owe you our apologies."

She was hovering in the doorway, along with her daughter and Governor Knox.

"I'm so sorry, Zo," said the Governor. "We should never have believed that you might betray us."

Harkman frowned, and Harry held his breath. Was Harkman going to scold the Governor of Vantia1, just like he scolded Harry when he forgot to do his astrophysics homework?

But in the end Zo's face broke into a sad smile. "Not at all," he said, gruffly. "Those images would have convinced me too. I've no idea how they were faked, or who did it, but—"

"It was Bremmer," Admiral Achebe interrupted. She was glowering with anger, and Harry was glad he wasn't on the wrong side of her. As she explained what had happened, Harkman's own face darkened.

"We searched his comms log," Governor Knox added. "He's been in contact with Vellis for months now."

Harry's ears pricked up. "What kind of communications? What did they say?"

Achebe shook her head. "Encrypted, of course. We've got our best analysts on it, but …" She trailed off.

"We'll keep working on it," said Governor Knox. Her hawk-like eyes glinted with determination. "For now, Harkman, your boy is to be congratulated. He destroyed another of Vellis's foul creations. And saved the station, once again."

Harry felt Zo's hands close over his shoulders and squeeze tight. Looking up, he saw pride written all over his guardian's face.

It was true. He'd outwitted Vellis once again.

So why didn't he feel good?

It was because the threat was still out there.

He couldn't help thinking of the strange transparent material that Bremmer had taken with him. Vellis had it now. Which meant that he might not be trapped in the Void much longer. He was free to come and go as he pleased ...

Sooner or later, Harry had a feeling he would be meeting Vellis for real.

And when that day comes, Harry swore ... *I'll be ready for him.*

THE END

Have you read the first thrilling
SPACE WARS book?